UNIVERSAL PICTURES PRESENTS A MOSAIC MEDIA GROUP PRODUCTION A JESSE DYLAN FILM WILL FERRELL ROBERT DUVALL "KICKING & SCREAMING" KATE WALSH MIKE DITKA MUSIC BY DAVID NEWMAN COSTUME DESIGNER PAMELA WITHERS CHILTON EDITED BY STUART PAPPÉ PETER TESCHNER PRODUCTION DESIGNER CLAYTON R. HARTLEY DIRECTOR OF PHOTOGRAPHY LLOYD AHERN ASC EXECUTIVE PRODUCERS CHUCK ROVEN JUDD APATOW DANIEL LUPI PRODUCED BY JIMMY MILLER WRITTEN BY STEVE RUDNICK & LEO BENVENUTI Mosaic THIS FILM IS NOT YET RATED DIRECTED BY JESSE DYLAN www.kickingandscreamingmovie.com DTS SDDS DOLBY DIGITAL A UNIVERSAL PICTURE UNIVERSAL ©2004 UNIVERSAL STUDIOS

1 2 3 4 5 6 7 8 9 10

❖

First Edition

kicking & screaming

THE COMEBACK KIDS

By Catherine Hapka

Based on the Motion Picture Screenplay

Written by Steve Rudnick & Leo Benvenuti

HarperKidsEntertainment

An Imprint of HarperCollinsPublishers

The Tigers were in last place.
They needed a new coach,
but nobody wanted the job.

Sam was the newest player on the team.

His father, Phil, spoke up.

"I will coach!" he said.

There was just one problem:

Phil did not know anything about soccer!

The Tigers took to the field.
But they did not know what to do.
"Do *not* just stand there," Phil called.
"Play!"
Each of the Tigers tried his best.
But the Tigers did not know how
to work as a team.
They lost the game by many points.

The Tigers were in trouble.

Phil needed to learn how to coach—and fast.

But first he needed to learn all about soccer.

Phil tried to learn soccer from reading books.
He tried to learn by watching videos,
but nothing helped.
The Tigers lost their next game, too.

Phil felt that he had to try something new.
I have got it! Phil said to himself.
He had a great idea.
A famous football coach named Mike Ditka
lived next door to Phil's father.
Maybe Ditka would help!

At first Ditka thought Phil was crazy.
"I am a football coach," Ditka said.
"I do not know *anything* about soccer."
But Ditka knew something important—
he was an expert on teamwork.

Phil talked him into it.

"All right," Ditka said.

"I am in."

He would be Phil's assistant coach.

At practice, Ditka gave the Tigers a pep talk.
"I am a coach who never gives up," he told them.
"Ever."

Ditka wanted the Tigers to eat, breathe, and sleep winning.

In the next game,
the Tigers tried to work together.
They even scored a goal.
It was their first goal ever!
But they still lost the game.

Ditka was not pleased.

"We have got work to do," he told Phil.

Ditka helped the kids work out.
He made them run in place.
He made them do push-ups.
He blew his whistle a lot.

But none of it helped.
The team was still terrible.
They lost their next game, too.

Phil was losing hope.

If Ditka could not help the Tigers,
no one could.

Luckily Ditka had an idea.

He brought Phil to a local butcher shop.

Two young Italian boys were working there.
Their uncle owned the shop.
During break time,
the boys played soccer with a wad of paper.
They were awesome!

The boys were named Gian Piero and Massimo.
(You say it like this: Jan Pea-err-o and
Mah-si-mo.)
Their uncle said they could play soccer.

Gian Piero and Massimo went
to the next soccer practice.
They showed the Tigers their moves.
They were amazing!

Phil and Ditka had a plan for the next game.
"Get the ball to the Italians,"
they told the rest of the team.
It worked—the Tigers won the game 18 to 0!

The Tigers were thrilled.
So *this* was what winning felt like!

More games followed.

The team followed the same plan.

The Tigers kept winning.

There was just one problem.

Nobody else was getting to play!
What good was teamwork
if only two of the boys helped the team win?

The Tigers made it to the finals.
But Phil could tell they were not very excited.
He made a tough decision.
"We should win or lose this
one as a team," he said.
"What do you say?"

Finally the Tigers looked excited.
Ditka had taught them about teamwork.
The Italian boys showed them
how to play soccer.
Now they knew what to do!
They played their hardest . . .

. . . and they won the finals!
The Tigers were the champions.
And they had done it together.